Return to the Sun

A Fairy Tale Adventure

LINDSAY SWANBERG

Published by Dragonfly Moon Press

ISBN: 9798666291009

To my beautiful, grown children
Fea and Ahja.

To all the children for whom I've provided
care and teaching, over the years.

To all the children of the world, may adults do
right by you. May you lead us into a kinder
future. Here's to you!

CONTENTS

DEAR READERS,

Is your magick listening?

May this story speak to your power within
you. May it heed this call. If it slumbers, may
this adventure wake it up.

We all have magick within us that longs for a
place to safely play.

Listen, when your heart sings, or when you
feel drawn to something in your guts. That is
your magick's way of speaking up and trying
to get your attention. Hear it and give it a
voice.

Only *you* can unlock your magick.

Chapter One

Warm woodsmoke from the fireplace drifted through the air in their cozy, old home. Josie's little brother, Hazel, napped on their fuzzy, worn couch under a thick wool blanket. It was his blanket that somehow always smelled to him like his sweet and loving mother. It smelled like oats and peaches and sugar and vanilla. The smell comforted him like no other. Especially since his parents had gone missing, four years ago. It was the most memorable thing he had left of her.

Josie had been caring for him this whole time - cooking for him, playing with him, keeping the house going for the both of them. Well, for them and their fluffy, orange cat, Honey. It had been a challenging four years, while they worried about their parents and lived in secret, but they had each other. They'd mostly gotten used to their new life, but still longed for their family back. They made do with their circumstances and had become the very best of friends.

You may be wondering how a 16-year-old girl had been caring for her eight-year-old brother for four whole years, now. How had she done it with no job, no parents, and living alone in secret? In part, she succeeded because it was her destiny. Deep in her gut, she *knew* it was her fate. It came naturally to her. The other answer to your question is quite simple *and* quite complicated, you'll see later in this adventure: Grandma Ruby.

Grandma Ruby was a welcoming older woman with long white hair and shiny dark eyes who owned the local bookstore. It had been Josie's favorite place to spend time, ever since her first childhood memories. She found something about it very soothing. Grandma Ruby - who wasn't actually anyone's grandmother, it's just what everyone called her- was often nice enough to let her stay for hours, on weekends and during summer vacation.

Josie would pour through books of all different genres, listen to adults enjoying some quiet conversation while they grabbed a cup of coffee at the back of the store, watch Grandma Ruby hang her dried herbs and say prayers over homemade candles, and take in with wonder her pet raven named Zhera. As a child, Zhera had seemed larger than life.

In her quiet kitchen, now, Josie daydreamed. She was remembering the day she realized something was wrong. The day her parents had gone missing, Grandma Ruby showed up with food, firewood, supplies for the medicine cabinet, Hazel's 4th birthday present, and the proof that magick is indeed very real. She came knowing Josie's parents were gone without Josie even having had time to go ask anyone for help. But before Josie could ask her how she knew, Grandma Ruby began reciting protective incantations over the house.

Josie watched in great awe as the air began to swirl in golden, sparkling, windless tornados, growing stronger as the chanting became more forceful. She *felt* the energy of the room pull upward, as if Ruby were conjuring the energetic flow of the very earth beneath them, giving their home roots into the planet's protective shield, and sending all that magick back up, out, and beyond the rooftop of their home. She wondered, for a moment, if the movement of forces had lifted her into the air as well. She had felt winged, for a second. Josie had been too distracted by Grandma Ruby's chanting to be sure.

It had begun in a remarkably foreign-sounding tone -Josie found herself startled by it, at first- but it quickly slipped into a ringing melody, like the song of a million birds calling for each other, the song of a deep cave awakening at its dark and hidden core, the song of every tree reaching for the sun, a song her spirit had always known and loved. She was moved by a sense of peace and strength that almost brought her to tears. She swayed and went somewhere within herself that she'd never known before. She touched a part of her inner world that she didn't want to leave behind, now that she had discovered it.

Eventually, she snapped out of the spell of bliss she'd been under and found herself sitting at their small, wooden kitchen table with Grandma Ruby and a mug of milky herbal tea in front of her. She could smell a chamomile-like aroma, with jasmine and rose. Flowers to soothe all beasts and brighten all storms. Its steam climbed upward like a dance in response to Ruby's song of power. Jo's insides were still dancing, as well.

"Josie."

Josie looked up at Grandma Ruby who had been watching her.

"Drink your tea, sweetie. It's going to help you process everything I have to tell you about . . . the *truth* of things."

As Jo sipped her tea, Grandma Ruby described their history of magick, capturing Josie's full attention in the realization that she was finally being talked to like an adult; *this must be quite important.* Hundreds of years ago, magick had been pushed back into the fae realms, from which it had originated, as power-hungry humans came into ruling this

Earth. They didn't want competition. Rulers wanted scared and submissive followers who didn't know magick, and didn't know that of which they were capable; they wanted followers who had no means of standing up to their rulers who had begun taking full power over them.

She explained that some of us still have blood ties to those magickal lineages, *the lineages of The Fae Folk*, but without the teachings of the old ways, without guidance, most of us just feel different and confused by the spark it ignites within us. Josie quickly pictured all the times she had felt a calling for something more within her gut. All the times she watched the sky change and the birds fly as if there were a message in these things. All the times she watched fire glide over wood, knowing there was an awake intelligence within the element.

Josie learned that day, on her little brother's 4th birthday, when she herself was only 12 years old, that her parents had disappeared under frightening magickal circumstances. While Grandma Ruby employed a search for them, she explained, Josie and Hazel's home would be completely invisible to everyone except for Grandma Ruby. No one would remember that either family or home had ever existed there. It was Ruby's way of protecting them, she proclaimed, until their parents could be returned to them.

So, Grandma Ruby brought weekly supplies and food. She left firewood for them and matches. She brought homework and access to online lessons, for them to continue learning in their captivity. *One must NEVER stop learning, after all. Learning is how we continue to grow and bloom.* She also brought Hazel a new scarf for his birthday every year.

They didn't live in a cold area, you should know. In fact, their town was often sunny. They lived in a temperate climate by the sea, where scarves and year-round fires in the hearth should've been completely unnecessary. Would've been unnecessary, for the average and normal family.

Hazel was different, though. *Special,* Grandma Ruby had said. Because of his ties to magick, in this world, he was always cold. Like his internal heat had been turned off. Even on his March 20th birthday; even later, in the middle of summer. He was always shivering and cool to the touch.

As a matter of fact, Hazel almost froze to death when he was an infant. That's when Grandma Ruby showed up, insisting he wear her hand-knitted scarves. Seeing that it worked, his parents went along with Ruby's "superstition," and Ruby became an instant friend of the family. It didn't take very many occurrences of Hazel forgetting his scarf for them to see how much he needed it.

As Josie finished making their lunch of sandwiches and soup, and stood there considering how much longer she should let her brother sleep, she had a flashback of last night's dream: her parents wandered through a dark, windy valley. A fire followed them, trying to catch up to them. They held hands, longing to find a way out and a way home to their children. It was a dream that had been replaying itself in Josie's memory all morning. The thought haunted Josie. What had happened to her parents? Would she ever know?

The phone rang, just then.

"Josie? Hi, Josie!" The voice on the phone said. "It's Grandma Ruby. I found your parents. I need your help. Can you come to the shop?" The line began to crackle and screech and then cut out completely. Goose bumps rose all over Josie's skin and the back of her neck began tingling like that of a kitten being picked up and dragged by her Mama Cat. Josie's breathing had quickened, too. She felt a shift of energy, like the day Grandma Ruby had conjured old magick in her home when she set a protection spell on it, except this time the energy was in her gut. She knew she had to follow the call within her that was telling her she *must* find Ruby.

So, she created a plan of action, while she took their plates of food to the table. She poured two glasses of strawberry lemonade. She opened the curtains to let some sunshine in, and admired for a moment the blue sky, the breezy green treetops in the distance, the small yellow bird watching her from their fence line. She took it all in, enjoying the quiet, allowing herself a moment of gratitude for her life, then walked over to Hazel and sat down. She got him up, gave him a long hug, and they headed over to their lunch.

"How long was I asleep?" He asked.

"Oh, just about an hour. I woke you up because something has happened."

Hazel examined his sister's face, showing awareness that she meant business. "What is it?"

"She found them. Grandma Ruby found mom and dad."

Hazel's eyebrows shot up. They began to talk excitedly about what this could mean, where they had been, how life could finally go back to normal once they were home. They discussed many of the things they had missed about mom and dad, Josie having a better memory of them than Hazel now did. They both wondered if they'd still be the same mom and dad, or if they'd come back different. Would things

RETURN TO THE SUN – LINDSAY SWANBERG

be the same?

While Josie and Hazel ate their lunches, becoming more and more excited about the possibilities, Josie explained to her brother that they had to go visit Grandma Ruby at the bookstore. She mentioned their phone call having gotten cut short. She didn't bother to describe the *knowing* she had within her that they wouldn't be returning to their house right away. After lunch, while Hazel showered and got ready to go, she packed a backpack full of supplies, just in case she turned out to be right.

Which, of course, she did.

Chapter Two

Josie turned the key in the lock on their front door. Even though no one could see her magick-protected house, the habit of locking it up every time they went to the bookstore felt reassuring to her. She put the keys in her pocket, adjusted the straps on her full backpack, checked to make sure Hazel's scarf was secure around his neck, and grabbed his hand to set off to Grandma Ruby's bookstore.

As usual, his hands were much cooler than they should be. They were also full of affection for his sister. There was no ignoring the way he looked up to her, and the way he adored her for caring for him. His bright green eyes twinkled in the sunlight and he pulled his scarf a little bit tighter, marching forward in the knowing that Josie always knew what she was doing.

He reminisced, as they set off, about all the games they had played together, all the art they had done, all the books she had read to him. She had even become a great cook, in all her meal-making for the two of them. She was his caregiver, but also his best friend. He pondered how kind she was with him, wondering if things were the same in other families.

From what he could remember, Jo was a lot sweeter than his parents had been. They were stricter and expected to be listened to; Josie, however, always took the time to patiently explain things and teach Hazel. She seemed to always have time and energy for long conversations and paying attention to the things that interested him. He admired her for that.

He also loved noticing their physical resemblances to each other. They both had soft, caramel-colored skin. They both had thick, dark hair. They both had bright green eyes. They were both tall. And yet, somehow, he felt … *different* from Jo. He felt … on the outside of her reality, somehow. Maybe it had to do with always being cold. Even with the fireplace blazing and the special scarves that kept him alive, he never felt warm. He struggled in ways no one else seemed to. He felt like an outsider, at the heart of things.

Hazel squeezed Jo's hand a little tighter. He hoped their relationship wouldn't change *too* much, with mom and dad coming back. He felt like he barely knew them anymore. Would they even be happy to be coming home? And Grandma Ruby – would she still be a part of their lives? He had grown very fond of her care, as well. He put these thoughts aside at the sight of a small yellow bird flying just overhead. It would fly to a rooftop of the shops surrounding them on their walk, watch them for a moment, then fly to another rooftop as if trying to keep up with them.

The walk itself was easy. It always had been. It was a quick stroll to Grandma Ruby's that Josie and Hazel had always greatly enjoyed. They lived in a quaint, beachside town near the main downtown street. It was full of cute shops and restaurants which attracted visitors. The sidewalks were lined with trees, potted flowers, and bike racks, and speckled with tables and chairs for café patrons, or coffeehouse regulars. Jo and Hazel went unnoticed, as usual -a side effect of their house's protective magick, they believed- strolling past all the stores and cars and friendly dogs on leashes. They loved the smells of cotton candy, and coffee, and brunch, and flower bouquets wafting through the air.

At the end of this downtown avenue ("Birch Street," if you plan on visiting anytime soon) that they'd been walking down, sat Orchid Park, with its benches and mermaid fountain full of pennies, with its old, towering oak trees and paths through the lovely rose garden. There lived Josie's memories of playing in the grass, lying in the shade, looking up through the oak leaves, as a child. Her parents loved this park and she had visited it often, before they vanished. She wondered how many of the pennies had been hers.

They veered left, to reach Grandma Ruby's bookstore, which sat just diagonally to Birch Street. Beyond it, if you continued in this direction, the street became highway leading out of their town, highway that shot past miles and miles of forest and foothills on the right-hand side and miles and miles of coastline on the left-hand side. Josie always loved the view, upon veering left to head to the bookstore. She couldn't imagine a prettier place to live.

Now, they reached the glass front door of the bookshop -the kind like one at a convenient store, where you either push or pull to go inside- and Josie gasped. Inside, she could see a terrible mess. That's not something Ruby would've allowed in *her* store. Furniture was overturned, with books scattered all over the floor, the lights were off at only 2:30 p.m. -scratch that: Josie could see the lamps had all been broken, not turned off- and Zhera was not on any of her perches. Josie pushed the front door open, with Hazel looking up at her in concern. They walked in to find claw marks on the walls and the glass cashier counter shattered.

"Grandma Ruby?!" Josie cried out.

She ran through the aisles of books looking for Ruby, looking for anyone.

Every aisle remained empty. Jo had a bad feeling growing in the pit of her stomach. And then she saw it: blood on the floor by the back door near the shelves where Ruby kept all her coffee and tea refreshments. Blood and black feathers, and the door was slightly ajar. Josie began grabbing the packets of almonds, granola bars, and cookies that were always stored with the drinks, and shoving them down into her open backpack.

"Josie, what are you doing?" her brother asked in confusion and surprise.

"We're taking these. Just in case."

"For what?" He asked her.

"We have to go find Grandma Ruby. This has to be about mom and dad, doesn't it?" She looked at him frantically.

Her brother shrugged.

"Yes," she insisted. "I know it is. We'll take some snacks with us, just in case we're out looking for a long time."

A noticeable shiver ran through Hazel. Josie thought it may just be his nerves, but she couldn't risk it. If he was feeling cold, she needed to help. She ran behind Grandma Ruby's cashier station to find her keys, and opened the cabinet with all the big porcelain coffee mugs. She quickly poured water from the hot water canister, into a big mug, over an orange spice tea bag. Mmm, the fragrance of orange and cinnamon.

"Here," she said, handing Hazel the cup of hot tea. Drink this while we walk. I've got a big bottle of water in my backpack for later, if we need it."

He took it, slowly. "Josie, doesn't this feel kind of ... scary? Something is off. Shouldn't we go get an adult for help? Maybe one of Grandma Ruby's customers who love her like we do?"

"We can't, little brother. You know that, right? They can't help us with this, just like they couldn't help with mom and dad. And we don't really have anyone else to ask, with Grandma Ruby's magick protecting us from everyone." It occurred to Jo, just then: *Oh, no. What if Ruby's magick doesn't protect us anymore now that something has clearly happened to her?*

"Besides," she said, looking into his eyes, "imagine going home and waiting for this to solve itself. We've been waiting for mom and dad for four years *and* now Grandma Ruby is missing." She took a deep breath and considered their options. "Does going home and waiting it out feel right to you?" She pulled him close in a hug.

"No. You're right. It doesn't. I trust you, so let's do this. Let's go look for Grandma Ruby." Hazel squeezed her extra, then opened the back door, the rest of the way, and led them out onto the brown and dusty dirt path that ran from the back door to the left of the shop, and parallel to the highway, for as far as they could see. It looked like it went on forever, from where they were standing. They both instinctively chose the direction the highway goes, feeling guided by the worn-in pathway, walking farther and farther away from town.

Walking along for quite some time, wondering where to look next if the path didn't take them anywhere, and merely relying on her gut telling her to keep marching, Jo began to recognize a peculiar feeling. Even before Jo's four years of having been invisible in her protected house, she had never felt so watched before now. She felt watched by the trees. She saw shadows shift amongst them, from afar. Something was in that forest they were headed towards. What it was, she couldn't tell, but she knew it was very interested in them.

Chapter Three

Finally, with aching feet, the sun having gone down, and concern that she had led them off into the distance for no reason, Jo and Hazel came upon a cottage. The path had taken them up into the foothills, winding up and around for hours, into more and more wooded areas, before they found someone's home. There were lights on, in the windows, and smoke spiraled up from the chimney -putting off the sweetest woodburning aroma Josie had ever smelled- and Hazel was quite certain he smelled homemade cookies in the air. A small yellow bird sat perched on the windowsill, on the side of the house, settling into its fluffed-up feathers, for the night.

Jo stopped walking. So, Hazel

stopped, too, and looked up at her.

"What is it?" He asked.

"I just . . . we're not really supposed to go to strangers for anything, but I have a good feeling about this place. Or maybe it's just because I'm so tired of walking. And it's getting dark outside. I'm not sure. I'm torn. But I feel like we should go here for help. Is that ridiculous?" Her stomach growled and her feet throbbed. She took out their water bottle and they shared the last few sips.

"I don't know," Hazel replied. "This place feels okay to me. And it *smells good.* And I'm tired of walking. And look! That little bird has been following us all day." He pointed at the yellow bird snoozing on the windowsill and Josie nodded.

"I saw her this morning on our back fence. I'm going to consider that an exceptionally good sign." She put their water bottle back in the backpack, adjusted it on her shoulders, and together they started up the stone walkway to the cottage. They breathed deeply as the fragrance of the lavender bushes that lined the house filled their nostrils. They heard music and laughter, radiating through the wooden front door, a very warm and inviting sound.

It caught Josie's heart strings by surprise to hear the sounds of adults enjoying each other's company like that: it had been *so long* since she'd heard anything like it. She thought of her parents and the family they had been together, years ago. She felt Hazel's watchful eyes on her and purposefully regained her emotional composure. She had to do this, after all.

Knock, knock.

The music paused and a moment later a blonde woman answered the door. She had a long, thick braid, to one side, with flowers in her hair. She had big, bright blue eyes, and pale creamy skin. She wore overalls and a tank top beneath them. Her feet were bare, and her toenails were painted varying shades of purple and fuchsia. The friendliest smile spread across her face and made her eyes light up like the moon and stars that were beginning to twinkle overhead. She was beautiful, and deep within Josie's inner world came the awareness: *she's special.*

"Hello! Josie and Hazel!" The blonde woman greeted them.

Their mouths dropped. They were too stunned to even look at each other. They searched her face for any kind of familiarity, but none existed for either of them. How in the world, they wondered simultaneously, did she know them?

"Grandma Ruby told me you'd be stopping by. Come on in!" She held the door open wider and waved them in. They followed her inside and were delighted by how cozy her home felt. It was warm, with so many soothing smells -wood on the fire, fresh flowers in vases by the front door, food in the kitchen, herbs hanging in large bunches on the wall nearest them to dry, and something magnificent that they couldn't quite put their finger on- that all blended together in a kind of perfect perfume, and they instantly felt at home. In an instant, their hearts felt saved.

"I'm Olive," the blonde woman introduced herself with a bow. "This is

Chloe..." she said pointing her open hand toward the other woman in the room. Chloe smiled from behind a table covered in musical instruments and music sheets. She smiled and winked at them, then went back to fiddling with her tunes.

She had a chiseled face, dark almond eyes, two black braids, and hazelnut skin. She went back to strumming her banjo, softly, immersed in the world of music she was birthing. She began to hum as she played quietly. Josie was struck by the peaceful energy that radiated from her; she found Chloe very mysterious and alluring. She wanted to know where Chloe's love of music came from, where had she learned to play these instruments? Did she live here? Where was she from? *Who are you?*

Olive guided them into the kitchen, instead, a lovely room with a stone floor, ceramic tiles lining the walls just above the countertops, handmade dishes stacked behind glass cabinet doors, potted plants hugging the largest kitchen window -a bay window- and spreading their green stems as if in a state of relief, and a big pot of soup that bubbled away on the stovetop.

Josie stared at the pot. She knew that smell. She and her brother locked eyes and smiled.

"Potato and cheese with a bit of broccoli and green onions!" Olive smiled, clearly cherishing her chef work. She began to dance around the kitchen, from sniffing the soup, to gliding to the cabinets for bowls and things, back to turn off the oven, and getting her boogey on while she prepared their dinner.

"My mom used to make that for us!" Hazel practically shouted.

"I know, honey. This is her very own recipe! I made it just for you. *And* we've got some cookies just ready to come out of the oven. I hope you like chocolate," she said with a sly look on her face.

"WE LOVE CHOCOLATE," they said in unison.

But at the revealing of Olive having known their mother, they looked at her quizzically, ready to demand answers.

How could coming here have been a coincidence? She saw it in their faces when she turned to look at them.

"Grab a seat at the table, my loves, while I dish you up some dinner and dessert. We'll have plenty of time to talk after you've eaten." She insisted.

Their noses, enchanted with the decadent aromas, persuaded by its scent of their childhood, a reminder of the times when mom and dad had actually been around, and their hungry tummies protesting the idea of waiting for food any longer, they decided that nothing sounded better than a good meal, in that moment. They sat, ready to eat, and ready to ask questions afterward.

One bowl, two bowls, a spoon in each. It looked so hearty and smelled so satiating! Olive added a sprinkle of fresh parmesan cheese on top, and placed a slice of warm bread smothered in butter and honey on the side of each bowl. They practically drooled as they watched her assemble their dinners. One platter of hot, gooey cookies, that Olive set down on the table in between them, and two tall glasses of cold milk. Two cloth napkins – one for each of them.

They dined in bliss, their taste buds exploding with joy, their hearts melting in comfort, their bodies settling in for the night. What kind of heaven had they stumbled upon? Jo chose to savor every moment, every aroma, every bite of food, every note of the music Chloe and Olive were making together in the living room, every crackle of wood snapping from the fireplace, for as long as she could, that night.

They sat swaying to the music, feeling fuller and fuller, enjoying the abundance and deeply thankful for the acceptance. Toward the end of their dinner, Josie stole a subtle look at her brother's eyes and body language, and savored the expression of peace and happiness on Hazel's face that she hadn't seen in years. He was able, finally, to enjoy a night of being a child. Josie hadn't realized, before tonight, how weary she had been, and how badly they'd both needed something like this.

She cleaned up their dishes and

invited Hazel to move closer to the fireplace in the living room, "You go ahead, Hazel. I'll be right there." When she looked over her shoulder, he had left the room. He was dancing in the living room and making up a song for the music. Jo paused to appreciate the bliss and relief she felt. *Thank goodness for good people.*

By the fire, they both danced. They spun each other around. They created funny new lyrics for old melodies. And the night flew by. Jo found herself sitting at the table with Chloe, who was teaching her all about music, the fire having died down to a bed of gentle embers whispering and crackling *good night,* when she noticed her brother had fallen asleep on the couch, his scarf hanging loosely from his neck. A glance up at the clock revealed the time to be almost 11:30 at night.

"Oh shoot, I'd better get us to bed," Jo declared.

"I can help you with that," Olive said, walking in from the hallway. "Follow me." She had pajamas in her hands, and towels.

Jo scooped her sleepy brother up - noticing that he felt surprisingly *warm,* for the first time in his life- and lugged him down the hallway into the guest room. After changing them both into pajamas, Olive tapped lightly at the door.

"Come in," Jo responded.

"Hi." Olive sat down on the bed next to her.

"Thank you for everything you've done for us tonight," Josie whispered.

"Oh, you're so welcome," Olive smiled. "You know, I've been watching over you and Hazel since he was a baby, ever since Ruby came into your lives..." Josie gave her a perplexed look. "I'm sure that sounds weird, since you haven't met me before tonight, but we've -Chloe and I- have been waiting for the right time to help you ever since your parents went missing. Well, before that, really. Ever since Hazel started getting too cold. Grandma Ruby explained it's because of his magick that he experiences that, right?" Olive asked. Josie nodded yes.

"Okay." Olive put her hand on Jo's shoulder and smiled. Jo's entire body felt like a pillow, suddenly. She was *the* most comfortable she'd ever been. "We can talk more later. I just wanted you to know that we're in this with you. We love you both." The feelings taking over Josie were like being in a hot bubble bath after a long, hard day, or like drinking hot cocoa on an ice cold day. She experienced peace and comfort in every fiber of her being. She quickly slipped into a restful sleep and Olive got up to leave.

Before closing the door behind her, Olive looked at the kids once more. They looked so much like their parents, she admired, yet they were so much more than just children. They were so much more than just mere humans. And if she and Chloe understood correctly, this sister and brother would save their world from the evil that had overcome it. They'd been waiting a very long time for these two to be ready.

Should she have told them that she was the one who took their parents? It wouldn't have helped anything: it was too soon to explain to them why, and it would just make them fear her and Chloe. No, she had done the right thing by keeping that a secret, for now. She really did love them. She just also needed something from them. Her whole world and all of its people needed her to set them on this journey. She would let Grandma Ruby explain everything.

She turned out the light and closed the bedroom door.

Chapter Four

When Josie woke, in the queen-sized bed that she and Hazel had shared the previous night, she lay reflecting on the evening they'd had in this lovely house. Sunlight pushed through the bedroom curtains, seeking to illuminate every corner and every shadow. Birds sang joyously outside her windows. The rest of the house, that she could hear from her bed, was still and quiet and serene. Josie basked in it, recalling their night.

They'd eaten the yummiest food they'd had in years, then danced to the melodies of Chloe & Olive for what felt like hours. The warmth of the fire embracing them, they'd lounged for the rest of the long and lovely night, talking and laughing and enjoying the sense of belonging that only good family can spark in you. They were naturals together, all four of them, like they hadn't just met a couple of hours ago.

They had discovered, that evening, that Chloe was noticeably quiet; she seemed kind, and observant, but aside from her music lessons, she kept to herself. Olive, on the other hand, was a bubbly person, and had treated them as if she'd always known them. They adored them both, immediately. During their music session, Olive would burst into song, serenading them, and filling their hearts with content and their bodies with ease. At the end of the night, she had shown them to their bedroom, she had loaned them pajamas, and she'd tucked Josie in.

Josie had instantly liked the soft

yellow paint on the walls, the oak bookshelf in the corner, the flowers on the fabric of the bedspread. This room was both cheery and cozy at the same time. Josie felt like she'd been there before. She had recognized something about it, but also knew she was way too tired to think anymore. Jo had set Hazel into their new, temporary bed, as quickly as she could, and climbed under the covers like a young child opens a Christmas present. She couldn't wait to dive into bed.

She remembered, then, the things Olive had said to her. She had fallen right to sleep while she and Olive were talking. She noticed the sense of stability it gave her to have a whole team on her side. She wasn't as alone in caring for Hazel as she had thought. And if they knew about his magick, surely this must mean she was one step closer to uncovering what that meant for them?

Josie had dreamed, that night, too, she recalled. She dreamed her brother had danced and danced until he frolicked right into the fireplace. She dreamed that his scarf protected him from catching afire, and she saw him morph -in the flames- into a dragon-sized bird of fire and take flight. It was glorious. His firelight spread, as he flew high above everyone, its glow lighting the world, until it shined into the valley of darkness that she'd seen her parents in last time. On fire -his soul's fire- he saved them from that world of fog and sorrow.

Hazel, however, had dreamed, symbolically, of being locked in a box made of ice. Everything around him withered in the freezing mist that seethed from his cold, frozen presence. He watched a world grow colder and darker, but he couldn't break free to run or to help. He watched shadow beings enforce this. However, surrounded by protective and powerful women, a root escaped him. It sprouted forth, pushing forth outside the view of the shadow people's. It was a survivor and it slipped past them without them noticing it. It came from his old magick, reconnected him to his light, and fanned the growing glow within him. His cage began to melt.

He laughed out loud in his sleep,

waking himself up, for a minute -letting go of his scarf and pulling the blankets off his torso so his warm skin could breathe- and he fell back asleep, reminiscing on the unusual heat last night's food had caused in his belly. He had *finally* felt some warmth within him and that delighted him back into a much more peaceful sleep.

Josie lay there, in the quiet, sunny room, her hands folded behind her head, witnessing her daydreams move across the ceiling, and starting to become more alert. She imagined what their next move might be. Would they continue trekking with no idea where they were going? A big part of her didn't want to leave behind this place and these people that she'd found. They'd already made a home in her heart.

Wait! she thought to herself, *Olive said Grandma Ruby said we would be coming. She MUST know something more about what happened to her!* Josie pulled herself up into a sitting position and turned, putting her bare feet on the cool floor. She tossed a glance over her shoulder and found her sweet little brother still conked out. The corners of her mouth spread into a grin. She sure loved him.

But time for some answers.

Pat, pat, pat. She could hear the pads of her feet making small pat sounds on the wooden hallway floor beneath her as she moved along it toward the rest of the house. It was quiet. She was worried to wake anyone, but excited to talk with her new friends more. Surprisingly, she noticed, she felt *restored.* She felt fortified. Being here made her feel stronger and healthier than ever. *I like this.* Jo thought to herself. *I could get used to this.* The living room was empty, when she got to it, so she went to check the kitchen: also empty.

The little yellow bird was watching her through the window above the kitchen sink, though, so Josie paused to say good morning. The bird tilted her head back and began to sing and flap her wings. Jo laughed as the bird did a little dance before settling back down to watch her. So, she made up a song in return for her:

Good morning

Yellow bird, like sunshine

Good morning

Little singer of mine

Happy day to you

Sweet winged one

Farewell my friend

Adventuring must be done!

She giggled, curtseyed, and turned around to find a kettle for tea. She grabbed a ripe pear from the fruit bowl and sank her teeth into its soft, juicy goodness. *Mmm.* She hadn't had a pear in years. Some juice trickled down her chin and she bent down to rinse her face under the cold water of the kitchen sink faucet. Going back to the fruit bowl, she found grapes, bananas, cherries, and peaches, as well. She rummaged through some drawers for a knife, found the cutting board, and put together a fruit salad for everyone. She added a fine drizzle of honey on top for an extra touch of decadence.

Jo decided to venture outside and see if she could find Olive or Chloe. They had to be here somewhere, right? *They wouldn't leave us all alone, here, right? They wouldn't leave without telling us?* Jo let herself out through the door in the kitchen that led to the backyard area. It occurred to her that upon walking up to the house, last night, she had not noticed Olive's expansive backyard garden.

For this being only spring, the growth in it was impressive! Olive had long garden boxes overflowing with kale and chard and winter spinach and garlic, bushes of nasturtium flower plants, tall and wide berry bushes, fruit trees that were beginning to blossom, and abundant bushes of rosemary, thyme, sage, and lavender. It smelled amazing back here. There were beautiful, handmade steppingstones lining the walkway of the garden. To the far back, there was a fountain in which birds splashed and chirped.

Wow, Hazel has got to see this! Josie turned back and went inside for her brother. He had woken on his own and had already come down to the kitchen. Tea was on, and the table was lined with pancakes dripping in maple syrup, french toast dusted in powdered sugar, roasted and herbed potatoes, fresh scrambled eggs, cream cheese danishes, an array of sliced cheeses with crackers, and her bowl of fruit salad. *Who did all this? It couldn't have been Hazel. Where's Olive?* she wondered, and smiled a hungry smile at her brother.

"Good morning!" He said. *Sleepy, but cheerful,* she noticed. *He's happy here.*

"Good morning to *you.* Look at all this great food!" They began piling up their plates. "Have you seen Olive?" He shook his head. "Chloe?" She asked. He shook his head again. "Huh. Weird. Well, I don't know where they are, so let's eat!" She poured him some tea and added a dollop of milk. They appreciated every morsel like it was their first meal in a long time.

"I want to show you the backyard. It's really beautiful," Jo said at the end of their breakfast. "They have this big garden that feels . . . extraordinary. Here, let's go get dressed, real fast, and then you can come see for yourself." They ran back to their room, put clean clothes on from Jo's backpack, brushed their hair and teeth, then put their shoes on. "Let me just look for Olive one more time, first." Josie headed into the hallway, putting her face up to the closed doors, "Olive?" Silence was her only answer.

"Is everything okay, Josie?" Hazel asked.

"I'm sure it is. I'm just surprised Olive and Chloe aren't here. I haven't seen a note or anything. And I only made that fruit salad; where'd all the other good breakfast food come from?" *They must be outside.* "Let's go see if they're out back. I want to show you their garden anyway. I would love to have one at our house. They're growing so much out there!" They reached the door in the kitchen and walked outside.

"Whoa, look at that!" Hazel took off running to see the tall, four-tiered fountain. It was topped by a giant pot of cascading jasmine flowers, out of which sprang a shining panel of stained glass featuring a bright golden sun. It was surrounded at its base by a deep, shimmering pool of water. When Josie caught up to him, she discovered iridescent gold coins on the floor of the fountain pool; they shimmered like rainbows. She grabbed one and put it in her pocket. She remained entranced, for a moment, until she noticed their yellow friend, preening from a tree just beyond the back edge of the garden.

"Hello, again."

"Chirp, chirp. Tweet, tweet." She spoke as she groomed her feathers.

"Hazel, I feel we need to give our birdy friend, here, a name." She looked down and saw that Hazel had wandered off. He had left the back end of the garden and was meandering through an orchard of apple trees. Birdy flew to one of them just past Hazel and began to sing. So, Josie caught up to Hazel and they both walked over to the apple tree holding their bird.

"Why do these trees smell this way?" Hazel asked, his nose in the air and delight upon his young face.

"Do you hear that?" Josie asked, taken over by the alluring melody of harps and flutes in the distance. She thought she could hear laughter and singing, and the humming of a melody she had heard before, along with the sound of the angelic music. It sounded like everything she had ever wanted to hear.

They walked, in silence, with Hazel's upturned face and Josie's buzzing ears leading their way. Something was calling to them, enchanting them, guiding them. Nothing could have stopped them from following their senses and the magick which pulled them onward. So, under a spell, onward they went.

Chapter Five

Hazel and Josie sat in a sparkling meadow, a little dazed about how they'd gotten there. Some kind of trance felt like it was wearing off, as Josie's thinking got a little clearer. Her brother had his eyes closed and a small smile curled upon his face. He looked like a kitten basking in the sun. Jo decided to let him enjoy the moment, for a little longer, and she began to process their surroundings.

They were encircled by a thin layering of tall, slender forest trees. The sky above them was a very pale rose pink, the soft golden sun comforting rather than blinding or harsh. Sparkles in the sky turned out to not be stars: they moved and danced through the air high above her. The earth upon which they sat smelled like cinnamon and firewood. Beautiful four-leaf clovers poked out from beneath them. *I've always wanted to see a four-leaf clover!*

She turned around, looking for the way back to Olive's house. There was nothing but trees surrounding them, though. No pathway that they would've followed to this meadow, from what she could tell. No dents in the bed of clover hinting at the direction from which they'd come. No idea where they were. Had she ever even heard of a clover meadow being out at the edge of town? *No. And I've never seen these kinds of trees before.*

The butterflies in her tummy picked up their pace and became a full-fledged sense of panic. Her heart began to race, her breathing deepened to catch up, her underarms started to tingle and perspire. It dawned on her that they also didn't have her backpack. They had zero supplies on them, not even coats or water.

"Hazel!" She tapped his arm, bending her knees to stand up.

"Huh?" He opened his eyes and looked around, more and more stunned, as he came to. "What the... where are we?!" He jumped up. "Josie..."

"I don't know, Hazel. Do you remember what happened to us – how we got here?" He shook his head and she continued, "I don't either. We were . . . walking . . . we were walking behind Olive and Chloe's garden. The bird. I saw the birdy, but what then? Music?" A chill gave her arms goosebumps, just then.

Clouds began sweeping in across the sky from behind them. Dark, violet, heavy clouds poured in on a fierce wind that blew Josie's hair away from her face and neck. Jo grabbed Hazel's hand and they began to run to the other edge of the forest, away from the storm, as the clouds opened and began their downpour. Running through the woods, looking for any kind of shelter, they found themselves running into drier, warmer territory with more and more trees surrounding them. Eventually, the earth shifted gently upward. The storm seemed to stay put far behind them, as they climbed the hilly ground.

Boulders began to mark their climb, the farther up they went. Ferns and mushrooms popped out of the soil.

Spiders skittered by and whispered hello. Owls hooted and sang out at them. The trees grew thicker in girth and in abundance. The woods, Josie noted, had gotten much denser. Their smell had grown richer and earthier, too. Much to her gratitude, after walking and climbing for several hours, they found a spring. Cliff faces now jutted up around them, as the hills had become mountains, and one of them had a clear, cold, delicious waterfall rushing off it.

Josie found bowl-shaped scraps of tree bark to fill with water and drink from until their bellies were full, their throats cooled, and their bodies hydrated. Stopping for a few minutes to swallow down seemingly endless amounts of refreshing water and rest their bones felt very peaceful for them both. They found some mossy stones to sit down upon, breathed deeply and relaxed, and got to take a better look at the new lands they'd navigated.

"I can see the meadow, Josie, LOOK!" Hazel pointed. Just barely in view, through trees far to the right of their path up the mountain, they could see the drop down to the clover-filled grounds they'd left far below. *What? How have we come that far? I don't believe it.* Josie stood up to go get a closer look.

"Careful," a familiar voice boomed from behind them. They jumped around to see who had spoken. They recognized her. "That ground becomes cliffside pretty suddenly. You didn't come all this way to fall to your demise," the tall, white-haired woman laughed.

"Grandma Ruby?!" Josie and Hazel both shouted, running to her and wrapping their arms around her. Ruby's long hair seemed to drift, suspended on a breeze neither Jo nor Hazel could feel, her entire being radiating a soft, golden white light. She seemed taller. She wore an ankle-length robe and held a long, twisted, wooden staff that was capped by a giant, sparkling chunk of ruby. There was a jade pendant suspended from a silver chain, around her neck. Little pieces of gold seemed to flicker and dance within the stone.

They stared in awe at their friend

and guardian. She was beauty, grace, force, and immeasurable fortitude. She was the wind that brings in fresh air and clears out old stagnation; she was the mountain on which villages could be built to last through the ages; she was the river to bathe you and satiate your thirst; she was the light of dawn to carry you into a new day.

"Ah, my dears, not quite. I *am* Grandma Ruby in your world. In mine, I am Gaia: She, Keeper of the Fae Forest. You have left your world and entered mine: the realm of fairies and other magickal beings! Finally. *Welcome.*" Her dark eyes burned with a violet flame. Josie felt the back of her neck prickle with magick. A sense of knowing, of recognizing, overwhelmed her being. She felt it wash over her, felt it take the reins of her spirit. She felt its infinite age -it timelessness- she felt her deeper self say, *"HOME. There you are. I've been waiting for you."*

"Grandma Ruby," Hazel looked up at her, comfort and relief clear in his sweet face, "Where are we? We've had the craziest time looking for you, and we don't really understand what's going on." Josie could see, also, fear in his green eyes. She hadn't realized how little she'd thought about his feelings, during everything they were facing. She wanted answers, she wanted to find their people, she wanted to follow the call that pulled her into this adventure, but she hadn't given much consideration to how her younger brother was handling all of it. She just wanted to get through it and be on the other side of it.

Josie was so tired of not knowing what had happened to her parents, not having a normal life with friends and school and family. And now, now there was so much magick involved in their lives. She was tired of feeling in the dark about everything. And what had happened to Grandma Ruby and Zhera the day she'd called Josie saying she knew where her parents were?

"We need answers, Grandma Ruby," Josie affirmed. Ruby's violet flame eyes twinkled back at her. "What happened to you at the bookstore? And what are we doing here? How do we get our parents back?" Josie removed her arms from hugging Grandma Ruby to step back and get a better view of her face, her body language, and any unspoken information Jo could pick up on.

"Josie, my love," she turned just a bit, to put her hands on Jo's shoulders, Hazel releasing his hug and listening intently to every word. "I have all the answers for you, I promise. But first, let me ask you: what do you feel, right now, my beautiful girl? In this place of power, in my true presence, what do you feel, here?"

She pondered the feeling of magick in her blood, breath, and bones. *HOME.* "I feel like I'm finally somewhere I belong. That I was always meant to be here. I feel strengthened by power and magick. It calls to me like it's mine. It feels like I'm waking up to something that has always been mine." Ruby nodded while Jo answered her. "What does it mean?" Josie was settling into the truth of the words she'd just spoken.

"It means ... welcome home, my

darling. Welcome home to your lineage, to who you really are, to your *future*." Ruby smiled.

"This is what's always been missing?" Josie asked, more realizing it for herself than expecting an answer that would change anything for her.

"Indeed." Grandma Ruby seemed relieved. Excited even. "Shall we begin?"

"Begin what?" Hazel asked.

Our initiations, Jo realized.

She turned to him, "Hazel, where's your scarf?"

Hazel and Jo both jumped, realizing they'd left it behind, somewhere. In the meadow? Would they have to go all the way back down there to retrieve it? *We'll need to bring some of this water with us... will Grandma Ruby go with us? I don't want to lose her again. Oh my goodness, did Hazel even have it on when we left, this morning?!* Their wide eyes stared at each other in disbelief.

"I . . . I don't know . . . I'm not . . .

I'm not cold," he answered in shock, looking up at Grandma Ruby.

"When did you stop getting cold, sweetie?" Ruby asked him. "Or an even better question, when did you start being able to make your own heat and feel it growing?" She knew the answer, but clearly wanted him to piece it together for himself. That's often the best way one can know anything, after all: through experiencing something for yourself and being able to connect the dots on your own.

"It was . . . back at Olive's house. She – I – ate her food and felt heat for the first time that I can remember. I don't think I've gotten cold since then!" His face was pure surprise and delight as a sense of freedom washed over him. "Am I cured?!"

"Yes, honey, hahaha!" Grandma Ruby laughed. "Yes, being back in touch with magick is curing you. *You* don't belong with humans, and that's why it was so dangerous for you." Josie shot her a perplexed look, but began to realize how much sense that made. *Our world was hurting him because it's not actually his world.* Jo wondered how she had not seen it sooner.

"Hazel, eating magick food has rekindled the light within you. You shouldn't ever have to deal with almost freezing to death again. Your return to the sun has begun. Jo, I suspect you've started having dreams that come true?" Josie blinked. *Is that what my dreams have been?* "This is the beginning of your initiations back into the magick you never should've had to live without in the first place."

"As for me at the bookstore," Ruby continued, "I was taken by the shadow people. They are the beings who've taken over the world of the fae. Let me explain. Shadows and darkness, in themselves, are not evil; these particular beings are, though, and they use darkness to spread and take over. They've been destroying the fae. The fae is the world of fae folk: fairies, centaurs, dwarves, and the like. Magickal beings."

Jo and Hazel looked at each other. They knew Grandma Ruby was telling the truth. They were having their eyes opened to a whole new reality. A reality they seemed born into. This was their birthright. Shocked, Jo and Hazel also felt quite excited to learn more.

"They caught me at my weakest: in my human form," Ruby went on. "They pulled me from your human world, thinking I was just a protector of your kind. Zhera was a bit frightened, and a little hurt in the process, but they didn't stand a chance with us; not here. This territory is *mine*. When they forced me back, here, I quickly overpowered them with my light, and they scurried back to their shadowlands: the lands they've taken over, that is. It won't be long before they come back with more of them, though. It's hard to fight them off when there are so many of them. That's how their darkness spreads. That's why we've got to go to the only safe place left: my home."

"We have a lot to discuss, dear ones, and a lot of preparing to do, to get you both empowered for that which is to come. But first, let's go eat and relax, shall we? I'll show you where I really live. Zhera is waiting for us." The shadows began closing in all around them, just as Ruby had predicted. Josie could feel them watching her, just like last night before she and Hazel had found Olive's cottage.

Jo and Hazel both nodded in agreement and great comfort that Grandma Ruby -that Gaia, Keeper of the Fae Forest- was here to guide them again. They took her hands and followed her into a shimmering bubble that had emerged to their left when they agreed to join her. Passing through her glimmering, light-filled portal, it felt like walking into paradise.

Chapter Six

Josie's Perspective

Hazel and I followed Grandma Ruby into her bubble – into her pocket of the world. She had created it for herself, we learned that day. She and her raven friend, Zhera, were its only residents, aside from the animals and bugs, that is. There were no other fae beings, here, and no humans, of course. She and Zhera resided alone. Zhera preferred that the open sky belong to her whenever she so chose. It recharged Ruby, too, to have quiet and peace surround her, she explained to me. Instead of being lonely, to her it was quite soothing.

Being so powerfully magickal, it was an easy feat for her to make her own safe land to live upon. It was work done in the blink of an eye. She still remained connected to the fae forest and magickal beings that she governed; she remained connected to our human world, as well. She was "in" all places at once. Like a multi-faceted prism, the light of life shined through her upon multiple realms, simultaneously. She held many worlds - and many lives- perfectly, in the palms of her hands. What she was capable of made human life seem so very, very limited.

Fortunately, for Hazel and me, she taught us a lot of it - or a lot compared to what we had known before her. We lived with her for months, fine-tuning our connection to magick and training our abilities to use it. With the right guidance, it came naturally to me. My ancestors were part Fae-folk, it turned out. Part fairy, specifically. Learning this explained so much about why I had felt so out of place, as a human, or like something was missing. Tapping into my fae lineage, brought forth that side of myself like it had always been there waiting to come out. It was my second nature.

Being in their realm, now, I uncovered that living without my magick had been similar to surviving on bread and water alone: so much had been missing! I simply hadn't known, before, what exactly was being hidden from me. Now, though, I was feasting on new wisdom and power. With Grandma Ruby's guidance and teachings, we really began to thrive. There's nothing quite as satisfying as getting to be who you really, wholly are. Being supported by loved ones, in your truth, is quite empowering.

Our time, there, was quite lovely, too. It was always a beautiful day out, whether we chose sunny or stormy; we always had nourishing foods, and enough high quality sleep to deeply rejuvenate us every night; we had both amazing lessons in power and relaxing down time to enjoy the stream, the meadow, the singing birds, the stars twinkling after dusk... it was a healing retreat after our hard, previous four years alone. It was also, I understand now, preparation for what was to come.

She taught us -almost daily- how to

hone our magick. Hazel's gifts had to do with heat and fire, while mine had to do with "the seeing." I learned I could "see" the truth behind things, could feel the way to go or not go, could dream of the things that were headed our way in our future, and could call things to us. The beacon within me that allowed me to pick up on the things no one else could, also allowed me to magnetize desired things and beings to us. I had an inner fire that burned to "see" and to "call forth."

*At first, I considered these things separate from each other: I thought they were two different gifts. In hindsight, I see that they beget each other. What's the point of being able to call forth into being the things that we want, if we can't also clearly **see** the whole picture? And what's the point of **seeing** the whole picture, psychically, if we can't adjust and assist the course of things for a better outcome for everyone? These gifts work much better when used together.*

Watching Hazel learn how to use his abilities, I finally came to see how different from me he really was. I'd always been his big sister, and then his only caregiver, and his best and only friend. I'd been too busy looking out for him and trying to make each moment the best I could for him, to pay much attention to his "other-worldliness." I had always been preoccupied with his health, too, and worried about keeping him from getting cold. Without that standing in our way, any longer, I came to fathom his strength, his force, his previously locked away potential.

Hazel wasn't human, I was realizing. He was far more than that. I was human with a magickal ancestry that gave me abilities – he, however, was a being locked in a human body . . . or something along those lines. In Grandma Ruby's care, I witnessed him learn to harness fire and control it as if he were one with it. He could even change the brightness and heat of the sun. We were never without light nor without warmth. Hazel learned to power Ruby's home and hearth, and even our sunny weather, like it was nothing. He could do it in his sleep. It's who he was. And it's why our parents had been taken from us.

I'll never forget the night Grandma Ruby sat us down to tell us everything ... well, almost everything. We had finished dinner, had cleaned up the kitchen, had gotten into pajamas. Out on the back patio, with our mugs of tea in hand, Hazel merely glanced at the stone fire pit and it blazed with a bonfire, instantaneously. He smirked and I giggled. That trick never grew old. Beyond the light of the flames, a dark sky housed the loveliest twinkling stars. A breeze moved through the air. Barn owls soared into the night. This had become my favorite time of day.

"Hazel," Gaia spoke, "You were stolen from your people. Your essence, that is, was taken away from your true form and put into Jo's little brother's human existence, in secret. The Shadow People bewitched you, in your original form, removed you from the fae, implanted you in a human family with no memory of who you really are, and surrounded you in magickal wards that made it impossible for others to come rescue you. With your light gone, though, all the light has vanished. The shadow people have been infecting the entire Fae world with pain, sadness, fear,

and suffering for decades. The darkness eats them up then spreads onto the next folks with any light left in them. It's destroying the whole world."

"Decades?" He asked. "But I'm only eight."

"In human years, yes, you are only eight," Gaia replied. "Fae time passes far differently than human time does, though. A hundred years can pass for the fae in one human year, or vice-versa. Fae time can be quite unpredictable, like that. For the fae, you disappeared over 70 years ago."

"How was I found?" Hazel asked. I sat there quietly, shocked by the truth that I was learning, but also eating it up. To me, though I wished the darkness on no one, this story was amazing. My existence was transforming before my eyes.

"Olive and Chloe. They are the last of the fae -the Sunfire Fae- who haven't been taken by the shadows because I took them in. I protected them, here. Then I moved them to Earth. I sent them to look for you and they were the ones who uncovered the

whereabouts of your human family. Because I had assigned them to be your protectors, they are the only fairy people who haven't fallen under the poisonous spell of the shadows that have been overtaking their universe."

Hazel looked down at his hands.

"There's more, my dear boy. Please stay calm when you hear this. You, too, Josie," she glanced at me. I nodded. "Remember that I love you and I've never wanted to cause you any harm. You are both very precious to my people. The truth is that Olive and Chloe did my bidding when they took your parents."

"When they WHAT?" He looked like he would explode into a massive flame. Or set this whole world on fire. I saw him struggle to contain himself and it looked painful.

"They're safe, Hazel. They're safe." Gaia responded with her hand up in the air to tame his anger, as if it somehow invited his rage to sit down. "We merely had to have the kind of leverage that would pull you out of hiding. The wards stopped us

from being able to come and take you home, so you had to come out on this journey of your own desire. Do you see that it was the only way?"

I pondered this. They had kidnapped our parents and forced us to live alone for years just to draw him out. But had they any other choice, with the wards in their way? I couldn't see any other options. Most importantly, it had worked. We had set out on this quest because of them and were now safely discovering who we are because of everything that had happened. The truth behind our lives had turned out to be so much richer than just unraveling where our parents had gone. I can't deny that it made me excited to be on this journey, and to look forward to many more adventures. I was also quite relieved to discover that they'd been taken by someone who I know would have kept them safe.

Hazel sat in a pool of his own sweat, breathing deeply, and keeping his blaze at a simmer. He seemed to understand why this had all been necessary and worked successfully to regulate his upset feelings.

"Yes, I see. There was no other way," he spoke.

"Your people, Oh Great One," Grandma Ruby continued to Hazel, *"are the Sunfire beings. You are the Sunfire King, ruler and guardian of light and fire."* We were shocked to hear this, of course. Well, I was. Hazel just nodded. I think something in him already knew and just needed to hear the truth spoken out loud.

"The Shadow People removed you to take over the realms. The lands have gone dark and cold. All the fae folk live in fear and sadness. We're going to awaken your inner Fire King, your true essence, so you can return to the sun. It is time for both of you to return to power. Do I have your consent?"

"Yes, Gaia, Great Keeper, Oh She." He said, a glow catching afire in his eyes. Something in him had changed. I nodded, of course. And with that, we began our training, began learning the Old Ways of the Fae Folk, and began restoring who we really were. What we would've done without Grandma Ruby, I will never know.

*She housed us, fed us, taught us, guided us, **loved** us, and healed us. Those are the kinds of gifts, in a person's life, that last with us forever. She was our rock from which we learned to fly. When her time with us was through, she granted us full access to our powers, for all the hard work we'd done. Hard lessons always hold a gift of newfound wisdom, don't they? Like little gems that continue to enrich us and reveal us to ourselves.*

Mine . . . well, my gift was that I gained my power animal. The yellow bird. She was my soul mate friend, in the fae animal world, which meant we belonged to each other. She asked me to name her, so I did. I named her Sunshine. I had, of course, also mastered psychic dreaming, and calling things forth into being. I felt like a new person – like the real me I'd always been meant to be. Connected to Sunshine, now, only fortified that.

Hazel's gift was a little more extraordinary, considering the truth of who he was: he could now unlock himself with ease. He remained in human form as desired, then exploded into light as The

Sunfire King when it suited him. One night, for example, he flew up into the farthest skies of the world Grandma Ruby had created, and he lit the whole dark night with the release of his soul. Bright light poured in through my bedroom windows, surpassing my thick drapes, warming my heart like a mother's most tender, embracing love. I felt cradled by his light and went on to enjoy the best sleep of my entire life.

But there was work to be done. We'd gone through all our lessons and trials, with Grandma Ruby, and had our gifts and power potential restored so that we could use those things to help the fae folk. We had to stop the shadow people from their painful reign. In my dreams, I had seen it. I saw the suffering our fae folk were living in, and how the shadow people fed off their energy and their fear. I saw the darkness. I saw the clinging residue of the shadow people, like a sticky grime they left on everything they touched. They were chaos, they were despair and giving up, and they were fear. They enveloped everyone in those things to take their power away.

Entrenched in this darkness, the fae folk turned against each other. Many had become agents of the shadow people, bringers of the darkness. They were either hiding in fear and sorrow, or inflicting suffering upon others. Beings who hurt others, after all, do it because they are so very hurt inside their own hearts. They think hurting others will bring them a sense of relief and restored power.

With the absence of light and hope, with the absence of community and kindness, the shadows spread. Fear and pain took over. Love lost its way and vanished. Life dwindled. The Realms of the Fae were dying.

I had seen it in my dreams, so I knew what was happening beyond a doubt. But I brought it up with Grandma Ruby, and she confirmed what I had come to understand through the dreaming: Hazel and I were the only hope for all of the fae. She unclasped the pendant that hung on a chain around her neck to put it around mine.

"Jo, listen carefully. Not much remains of the sunfire essence, since the

King's light disappeared. Most of what does, lives in this pendant for safe keeping. Guard this with your life, but use it whenever your magick needs a boost. I have a good feeling it will help you get through the darkness." Gaia said to me gently.

I rubbed the jade between my fingers, watching the golden flecks swim and dance within it. They moved in sync with my touch. My fingers quickly warmed, and the pendant began to glow.

"Oh! It likes you." Ruby laughed. "I knew it would. Best not to unleash its powers just yet, though," and she tucked the pendant beneath the top of my shirt.

This was our last day in her home. We three savored some breakfast toast, oatmeal with nuts, bananas, and berries, and chamomile tea. Then Hazel and I got ready. We were meant to save magick from evil. It was our sole purpose, now. It was time.

Chapter Seven

Josie and Hazel had set out from Grandma Ruby's world in high spirits. They knew what they were meant to do, they felt inspired by their powers and abilities, and they were excited to save the fae. They couldn't wait to see their parents again! How excited Jo was to get her family back.

She wondered if Hazel felt the same way, or if he would only care about his Sunfire family now. That was a real possibility, she realized, and it would be understandable. She didn't want to lose her brother, but she would accept their fate, whatever that turned out to be. They left Ruby's realm excited, brave, and hopeful.

The fae forest seemed just as they had left it: warm, breezy, densely wooded, the spring pouring joyously from mountain to pool below. Josie took a taste, before continuing on, but spat it out immediately.

"Don't drink the water, Hazel!" She put her hand up in a s*top* position, hunched over and spitting. "There's something wrong with it. Let's stick to using the bottle we packed. I don't know what happened to it, but it's not the same water as before."

As they began to hike away from Gaia's, Josie considered their supplies: Gaia had given them a jug that had a magickal filter for providing them with clean water, and they had powdered sunfood. Adding a little to some water, they could make filling and nutritious meals. They had more than enough to get them through their mission. They had sleeping bags and a small tent, if needed. With Hazel's ability to control the surrounding weather and temperature, though, she wasn't sure they'd need the tent for anything. They brought it, just in case, because Gaia had wanted them to.

Gaia had also given them instructions to follow to get to the heart of the darkness as safely as possible. They were strictly forbidden from entering any caves, for one thing. She'd warned them they would be serving themselves up on a silver platter for the nastiest of little gremlins, if they didn't avoid the caves. They were to stick to the worn, dirt pathway, following the downward flow of the river, until they could see the villages in the valley below. Heal the villages, she had told them, and all the other fae would follow suit.

In the distance, shadows sneered. They blew whispers of discouraging words in on the breeze that whooshed through Josie's hair and into Hazel's lungs on his every inhale. The light in the pale pink sky, which emanated from Gaia's world, wouldn't last much longer. Jo could see, not far in the distance, where the light ran out, and shadows had engulfed the rest of the world.

Jo and Hazel marched along, the pep dying back from their step, the growing darkness of their surroundings clinging to them like wet cobwebs. It beat down on them, in tiny, malicious, harping beats, ever unnoticeable, permeating the quiet back of their minds. The darkness itself conveyed to them that they were tired, convinced them this trek was useless, weighed their hearts down with longing to give in.

The sun was setting, they were exhausted -and, secretly, they both felt a bit defeated- so they decided to set up camp for the night. Hazel instantly found that his powers had diminished here, so close to the shadows. He could make fire, but struggled to control the cooler air and evening wind that had been picking up with the onset of twilight. So, they picked a spot closer to the mountain, that jutted up on the right-hand side of their path, for better wind protection.

Fallen tree branches and twigs were

easy to come by, so building a small fire was an accomplishment Hazel set out to enjoy. He made an upright triangle out of the wood he had collected, standing it within the circle of stones that Jo had arranged, and he smiled as everything in him tingled and the wood caught fire. They both stood, appreciating the crackling campfire, for a moment. They moved any remaining rocks to the outside of their camping spot and lay their sleeping bags down.

Jo quietly got out their small pot and some filtered water to boil. The powdered sunfood thickened in it rapidly. She dished it up, for the two of them, and sat watching the stars begin to twinkle with each bite. Her belly grew warm and happy.

"Do you feel that, in your belly, Hazel?" She looked at her brother. He'd fallen asleep at the end of eating his food. She set her bowl down and smiled. The sunfood seemed to have restored some of her bright spirits.

I wonder how long this will last for. I was starting to feel pretty miserable earlier, but this has helped. Goodness, how has everyone here been living with this darkness looming over them for so long?

Nourishment in her stomach, and sleepiness in her bones, she stretched out on her sleeping bag, next to the small, wonderful fire. She took a few deep breaths and got comfy. Looking up at the lovely night sky, she caught a few shooting stars whizzing by, before she dropped into sleep, like her brother had.

Jo dreamed. She saw her parents in the valley of shadows. They were stuck, unable to see, unable to hear, unable to find their way out. Flames arose behind them, warming them, rescuing them from the dark, and illuminating everything around them so the whole world could bask and thrive in its glow. It was like the most brilliant dawn struck them and saved them from sinking farther down into the gut of a hungry, unending abyss. Her parents saw her in the light.

"Josephine?" Their happy, teary eyes took her in.

"Mom? Dad? It's you!" She said in

her dream.

She heard someone screaming, but didn't want to look away from her family, who she had *finally* found.

Screaming. It wasn't in her dream. Hazel was screaming. Jo sat upright in the dark, terrified to hear her brother screaming. It was pitch black. No campfire, no moon and stars. Just pure black.

"What is it? Hazel?" She yelled for her brother.

"Jo! They're eating me!" He conjured a small flame that revealed they'd been moved into a long, dark cave tunnel and Hazel had small creatures biting into his legs. They were covered in fur and spikes, with tiny eyes, leathery paws, with large, very sharp claws, and long pointy teeth that were dripping.

Jo stood up, her hand going right to her pendant, and she called for protection. Silently, at first, she called for the gremlins to leave. Instead they continued to gnaw on Hazel's bleeding calves and shins. He screamed. They were taking whole bites out of his legs, and she could see black lines moving up his legs from the bite marks. The more energy she sent to her call, the more her pendant began to glow. She merged with the heat it was producing and felt light course through her veins.

"I SAID I CALL FORTH PROTECTION. NOW. COME TO US. PROTECT US." She bellowed. Hazel was shocked by the change in her voice -the change in her power- and he savored both the inner Sunfire King's enjoyment of watching her bloom *and* his own eight-year-old, younger brother pride. His sister was AWESOME.

A giant, invisible hand reached out in the clammy, cold tunnel and scooped them into its palm. It pulled them into the rocky, clay wall and covered their mouths. They felt it whisper *be quiet* to them both. The gremlins screeched hysterically for their food, and began sniffing the ground, sniffing the walls, hitting each other, and furiously throwing stones off the ground. Eventually, they left to go back to their hunt for dinner.

The invisible hand released them. Hazel fell to the ground, crying. He cried out for Jo, quietly, to avoid drawing the critters' attention again. His stomach swam with nausea. The smell of his blood filled the air. He felt a sickness radiating from the bites. Jo's pendant throbbed with light and heat. As it grew brighter, she could see the horrible condition her brother was in.

"Jo, it hurts! Oh my god, it *hurts*. It's taking over me. Help me!" He squirmed on the floor of the tunnel.

"He has been poisoned. It's how they get you. They feed from you then turn you. Your brother will become one of them if you don't stop the poison from spreading. I'm sorry I cannot help you. I am too weak. I am hibernating." The voice of the hand was deep, old, and powerful, but sleepy.

Jo ran to Hazel, propping him up in her lap. She put her pendant on his left leg and called forth his healing. Then she did the same with his right. She called on the poison to leave his body. She called on his immune system to fight it off. She called on his heart to force it out of his bloodstream. She called on his cells to armor themselves against the poison. And she called on the sunfire light within her amulet to save him.

A flash of light exploded all around them, making it too bright to see anything. They squinted their eyes closed. They were suspended in healing white light, without weight, without need, without time. Then it passed. And reality returned. They sat on the cool, musty earth. Hazel's wounds were clean and closing, and the sickness lines on his skin were gone. His ability to glow had returned, which was helpful in the dark, but everything else was black. Jo wondered which way was out.

"How did we get here, Jo? The last thing I remember," Hazel murmured, "is that we were eating dinner. I think I fell asleep at dinner."

"They dragged you in," the voice spoke. "You must not sleep near the caves like that. That was an awfully close call. I've seen them…" his voice became sad, "I've seen them eat so many helpless beings, and there was never anything I could do to help."

Jo thought through the many questions she had pouring into her mind.

"Who are you?" She chose to ask first.

"I am Lou. I am the Keeper of the Mountain. We are hibernating. So, I don't have much power," he answered. There was a kindness in his voice that Jo liked very much.

"We are hibernating? Who's we?" She asked Lou.

"My people. We are mountain giants – *peaceful ones,* have you no fear! We must hibernate for thousands of years to restore our energies. We are guardians. We have become one with the mountains while we sleep. I am the leader of my people which is why I was able to wake when you called for me. But there's not much more I can do besides making you invisible within the cave walls. Gosh, I'm so glad you lived. And you - you are a Sunfire Guardian, I see from your amulet."

Jo beamed. "Yes, I suppose I am." She hugged her brother and stood up.

"Lou, thank you so much for helping us. Is there any way I can repay you?" She asked him.

"Restore the light, dear one. That is all I ask." Lou answered.

"We're working on just that," she smiled.

"There is one other thing," his voice had grown much softer.

"What is it, my new friend?" Jo nudged him.

"The coin. In your pocket. From the sunfire fountain at your cottage. If I may have it, I would be able to call upon you in your human world when I have completed my hibernation." He sounded embarrassed to ask.

"Absolutely," Jo smiled. "It's yours." She dropped it into his enormous palm, and it disappeared from her sight. Something about that action had felt like the right thing to do. She suspected she had a *knowing* happening that she wasn't allowed to fully s*ee* just yet. For the future, she listened to her gut.

"Lou, if you can make us invisible for the rest of the night, would we be able to stay here with you so we can get enough sleep to set out on our journey again tomorrow? I don't want to go back to our campsite and have a repeat of what just happened."

"It would absolutely be my honor." Lou scooped them up into his massive palm, once more, and they slumbered peacefully like two baby birds in a nest.

Jo dreamed again. She saw into the distant past, in which Lou and his tribe of peaceful giants protected the lands. They were 20 feet tall, some of them winged, all of them with the most captivating singing voices. They were tree farmers and dragon whisperers. They had erupted foothills into greater mountains to provide shelter and shade from the elements. And, as guardians of the fae, they were the first under siege from the darkness. The shadow people had forced them into hibernation. In Jo's dream, she *saw* that

The Sunfire King's light would awaken them.

She woke in the night with a realization. *This is not the only realm affected by these shadow people. They are eating away at all the worlds.* She stroked her brother's cheek, s*aw* what their future could hold, with his return to power, and fell back into a more restful sleep.

Chapter Eight

In the morning, Jo and Hazel stretched. They could see a small amount of light at one end of the tunnel. Wow, those little monsters had really dragged them a long way. Jo cringed at the thought of them. Hazel's stomach rumbled for breakfast. Jo thought of their supplies: would everything still be there? They climbed off the squishy, warm palm of their new friend.

Hazel hugged and kissed Lou's giant finger and said, "I won't forget this, my friend. Your people will be remembered and rewarded." His voice barely sounded like his, Jo noticed again.

"My King? My King, is it you?! You have returned for us! I *knew* you would.

Oh, we are saved." Lou rejoiced.

"Don't spread the word just yet," Hazel patted Lou's hand. "Let us make things right first, okay? We still have a lot of work to do, to return to the sun and remove this infection of darkness. Extra attention from the shadow people will only make that harder on us." Hazel sounded more certain of himself than ever.

And so, they started out, once again, ready to save the world -worlds, as Josie now understood the truth of things to be. It wasn't just this world; it was worlds, plural. At the end of the long cave tunnel, Jo was thrilled to see their belongings still heaped all over their camp site. Hazel was dismayed to see that more of Gaia's pink sky light had been absorbed into darkness. The sky wasn't right, out here. It was morning, but the feeling of day versus night had disappeared. Now, there was only the fading of light and the void its absence left behind.

They sat for tea and their sunfood "oatmeal," trying to share positive thoughts with each other. They discussed the adventure that lay ahead of them.

Josie told Hazel all about her dream and what the giants had been like. Then they packed their things, unknowingly having lost all interest in talking or laughing, and set out on the rest of their quest.

Jo and Hazel trudged along the path, steering clear of any cave mouths in the mountainside, walking quietly for hours. Every once in a while, Jo would look down to check on her brother, but he kept up just fine and didn't seem to want to talk either. Things had grown much darker - or was she just imagining things? No, she wasn't. Everything around them had changed.

I don't have very much energy anymore. Jo daydreamed. *I mean, I did. In the cave. I loved meeting Lou and dreaming about his people, last night. I want to come back to him when we fix everything. He's my new friend. I want to befriend his whole tribe. Why does it feel like we won't make it? Why does it feel like we should turn back? Can we? Can I just go home and rest and not worry about this anymore? It's too far. Everything is too far away. Nothing matters.*

They plodded along, doing their best to follow through on the purpose they'd been given. Then hours turned into days. And days turned into weeks. They only stopped to drink water, make food, and sleep, when they just couldn't go on any farther. Any sense of time had faded into nothing. They ate when hungry and slept when tired, but had no other sense of direction guiding them. They kept their course by staying on the dirt pathway they'd been told by Gaia to follow.

Every step felt like moving through quicksand. Their muscles were heavy, their minds burdened with every doubt they could possibly have about their mission. It was as if every fear they could have about not being strong enough or good enough crept into their minds. Their hearts had become riddled with worry and defeat. The shadow people snickered and mocked them from the darkness.

When had their inspiration faded into . . . something *else?* Hazel couldn't remember clearly. Jo couldn't put her finger on it. They'd been traveling for . . . *how long?* Past the mountains, avoiding the caves, along the downward flow of the river – just as Grandma Ruby had instructed them. Their feet, though, and their legs had become so heavy, at some point along the way. Their backs arched, and their heads hung low. They had food, their magickally filtered water, they had campfires and sleep . . . but nothing revitalized them. They just felt so *burdened* by the weight of being alive.

The farther they went into Fae Forest, and the closer they got to the villages that housed the fae beings, the harder it got to want to keep going. The murkier their memories became. The heavier their hearts grew.

Why are we doing this? It's pointless. Everything hurts. It isn't worth it. They kept going, day after day, into deeper and darker territory. There was no sun, no stars. During the day, the woods seemed barely lit by some ice cold, light blue iridescence that didn't quite seem to have a source.

It was eternal night, without the beauty of dusk, without the mystery of a starry sky, without the awakening of nocturnal beings who were grateful to stir in the night, without any hope for dawn. It wasn't just dark and cold, though: it was empty. It wasn't the kind of night on which you'd want to cozy up by a roaring fire with a hot mug of cocoa. It was . . . a void. An empty, infinite void of nothingness, with an appetite. The emptiness longed to eat whatever good and warmth and light you had left in you.

How long has it been? Josie wondered to herself. *Does it matter? Does anything matter? It did when we left.* She thought back. *It's been two weeks? Three, perhaps?* She pictured Grandma Ruby's face, but it was distant – like a long-lost dream from her childhood. It was hard to connect to.

And then she saw it, what Grandma Ruby had called the heart of the darkness: the villages in the valley below. They had come so far, had pushed through the wall of despair that did everything it could to bring them down, and they had finally arrived so close to their destination.

But the darkness had seen them, too. It had finally *seen* them through the eyes of its servants, the shadow people. As Hazel and Jo had slowly plodded along, dedicated to marching step by step until they could physically go no farther, some creatures watched them and realized they were more than the typical fae they had overtaken.

"WHAT is a *human* doing HERE?" One of them asked, with shock and disgust, in their old tongue. In English, we would translate the name of their language as something along the lines of Skritskrit.

So, in Skritskrit -which sounds a lot like a nasty blend of hissing, clicking, and combining too many consonants together- they questioned as to how these two had survived their constant onslaught of darkness against them. How did a human get here, in the first place? And what even *was* the little boy?

"Oh, no. No, no, no! It's THEM! It must be," the eldest cried out.

"Who, my lord?" the younger ones spoke in unison.

"It's *the Sunfire King, after all this time, and his Guardian!* We must get them. We must change them or they will be the end of us all! Go! Give them everything you've got!" He ordered.

They tore forth from the trees, running at full speed, screeching and howling, emitting the maximum level of despair and negativity and fear at Jo and Hazel that they could muster within them. All things that live long to survive, after all. Even the evil things.

Jo heard them, in the distance. She s*aw* what it would mean if those creatures caught up to them. She knew their mission would be over and would have failed. She couldn't let that happen.

"Hazel, RUN!" she commanded. Instead, he plopped down and was lying on the ground, helplessly.

"I can't anymore, Jo," he whispered. I can't go on. I *want* them to eat me. I'm done. It's okay. It will feel good. It will make me feel better to be one with them." Jo's jaw had dropped, but she could hear them closing in on them. They had to move. *Fast.*

"OLIVE!" she called out as she bent over and scooped up her heavy brother. She tossed him over her shoulder to get the best grip on him. She was just going to have to carry him.

"OLIVE, CAN YOU HEAR ME? I NEED YOUR HELP!" She yelled and began running as fast as she could. Fortunately, she was much stronger than a purely human teenager would have been. She was part fae and she had become a Guardian. Running was difficult, especially with the added darkness seeping into her, but she had to keeping moving.

The monsters following them were keeping up with them, she could hear. If she tripped up even once, they'd be on them both in a heartbeat. This was it: escape them now or this whole journey would end in the worst way possible.

Suddenly, in response to her call, a bubble of light -almost blinding, in this darkness- opened ahead of her. It was a portal. Two young-looking, winged fairies came running and laughing toward them. A flowering meadow and sunny sky lay behind the fairies.

Jo was so shocked by the light, she could barely see and process everything. So, she kept running. Before she knew what was happening, Olive and Chloe in their lovely, true fae form, but appearing as children, ran up to her, holding hands, and kissed Josie on each of her cheeks. They flew alongside her.

"Remember your gifts," their fairy voices tinkled in her ears. "We cannot stay long or the darkness will take us, too. We can hold the creatures off for just a bit, though, to give you a better lead. Take this bit of light to help!" And they blew a small flame of Sunfire essence from their hearts into hers.

She saw, as she glanced over her shoulder, the shield they erected behind her with their fairy magick. The light kept the creatures in the distance as Jo hauled Hazel on her back at the fastest speed she could go. Her amulet began to pulse along to the rhythm of her own heartbeat. The sunfire essence was helping.

She fought to hold onto what her fae friends had said: *remember your gifts. My gifts? My gifts: I see. I call things forth,* she remembered. Now her head pounded. Critters began to call her name and snicker to each other from the caves in the mountainside. They must've been alerted to everything taking place. *Is the darkness connected to everything, too? Like the light is? Keep running,* she encouraged her weakening legs.

She could hear the gremlins running after her, in the mountain terrain, their hungry, threatening teeth chattering, and their claws scarring the boulders across which they scurried in pursuit of her and her brother.

I see things! I call them forth! I AM THE SUNFIRE GUARDIAN, BRINGER OF THE LIGHT.

Jo was out of breath and her legs wanted to buckle beneath her, but she kept going. Ruby's reminder sounded in her heart, "Remember who you are, Jo. RE-MEMBER." *Remember . . . I see. I call things forth. I am here to restore the Sunfire people.* The darkness beat more heavily upon her heart making her grimace in searing pain.

She imagined Grandma Ruby, as she ran, slowing, but still forging ahead; she imagined Chloe and Olive; she imagined her parents. She imagined the joy of having everyone home, again, safe and sound. The Sunfire flame within her grew and warmed her and cleared her head.

She breathed deeply, remembering her time with Gaia, letting the sunfire fully ignite within her, fueled by the strength of the amulet's essence, dissolving the cage of darkness that had clung to her heart so ferociously. She let it in and returned to her power.

"HAZEL," she called to her brother. He flinched, huddled over her shoulder, and crying in his deepest agony.

"HAZEL. OH SUNFIRE KING, I SUMMON YOU. I COMMAND YOU. COME FORTH." She put her hands up, gripping the energy of the ethereal strings that connect all of us to life.

"COME FORTH, OMNIPOTENT KING OF THE LIGHT. IT IS YOUR TIME. COME FORTH *NOW*." She breathed and pulled on the strings with more focus and force.

Her power had replaced the weight of the shadows, though she still stood surrounded by the darkness of the void. The creatures retreated, though, realizing they were too late. Realizing they were now the ones in danger of her strength. Her power was drowning out the sadness and fear surrounding them all, dissolving the grief that was eating this world alive. She called on The Sunfire King to come back to himself.

Hazel looked up, a fierce orange flame in his eyes. "Josie? My dearest friend, *say it again*." He stood up, slowly, weakly. As she called him forth, he began to vibrate with power and energy. His skin began to glow. His veins became visible, appearing as lines of brilliant, golden light within his flesh. His sunfire was activating.

"SUNFIRE KING, I CALL YOU FORTH, INTO YOUR TRUE BEING. INTO YOUR POWER. NOW, MY KING! RETURN

TO YOUR PEOPLE. *RETURN TO THE SUN!"* Josie's voice shook the earth and trees around them.

The darkness had fallen silent in awe. It fell away from them as the fire radiating from Hazel's body glowed stronger and stronger. With that, The Sunfire King left Hazel's body (which fell to the ground, instead of morphing into the Sunfire King's transformation, as it had always done before) and he flew to the sky, bursting into flames.

The entire world was suddenly illuminated. The sky was bright again. The lifeless, blue iridescence of the forest was instantly gone. Any remaining shadow critters ran away, screaming, as if the brightness of day hurt them. The trees stretched and reached for the light, gasping and rejoicing in their first sense of joy in years. Flowers sprang forth, having been awaiting this return of goodness. Birds sang, once again. The fae folk squinted.

Sunshine flew to Jo's shoulder - *Goodness, how had I forgotten you, my best friend? How did I forget you in the shadows?* They sang birdsong to each other, for a moment. They sang, "Hello, how are you? I love you, too."

It was *so good* to be back. The light of the Sunfire King washed over them, kissed them, held them, emboldened them. Sunshine and Jo looked each other in the eye and, knowing what was needed next, they consented on morphing.

"But first . . ." Sunshine said, "I must show you the truth." She put her forehead to Jo's and made Josie *see*. In her vision, Josie saw where these shadow creatures came from: they were the by-products of humanity's deepest fears materialized. As magick had been forced back into the world of The Fae, so had humanity's darkness been manifested as evil beings, here. Human people had not only forced magick out of their world, but their lengthy history of negativity -their violence, their fear, their greed, their hate- had also created a disease that had spread within the realm of the fae folk.

Jo extended her arms in bird pose, as she had been taught by Gaia to do. She lifted her face to the sky. She lifted her right foot and rested it on the inside of her left thigh -the position for morphing. Sunshine flew up into the air, circled around, brewing her magick up higher and higher, then shot down, in a whirling golden light, into the center of Jo's chest. They became one, this magickal way, and Jo spread her new, big, beautiful yellow wings. She soared into flight, heading for the fae villages below.

The fae folk were fleeing their homes, astonished by the light and warmth now bathing every fiber of their beings. They ran to see the source. Many of them fell to the ground in agony or crouched down staring up at the Sunfire King in desperation. Jo *saw* the last of the shadow beings hanging onto the very hearts of the fae folk. They had permeated their spirits too deeply and for too long to be kicked out that easily.

She watched the fae folk struggle and cry out for freedom as the shadows fought to override the light with their suffering. All of them: the village faeries, the centaurs of the hills, the dwarves of the mountains, the mermaids of the waters... they all fought to shake off the shadow creatures who had taken up residence within them. The Sunfire King already shined upon them as brightly as he could.

Jo flew over town after town, the Sunfire King's radiant light healing the lands, healing the gardens, the Fae Forest, the animals, the waters, *calling* to each magickal being. Remembering the energy and magick within Olive and Chloe's music, she called forth their song and their strength and the support of their lineage of ancestors who had come before them.

She called forth their resilience and their joy and their gratitude, through song. The darkness screamed and withered. The shadow people sank their claws deeper into the fae folks' hearts and so she called to them next.

"I call you forth, shadow beings. RELEASE MY PEOPLE. I call you forward and out of their hearts. I COMMAND YOU: RELEASE THEM AND COME FORWARD TO ME." She pulled them by the strings within their souls that connected them to the web of life. One by one they drifted up to her, reluctant, but powerless against her call. They screeched as she pulled them into the light.

"Now sing, People of Fae Forest, SING! SING the love back into your hearts where it belongs. Sing the hope and the joy and the peace back into your souls!" Josie's amulet pulsed with their singing. She felt it pound like a racing heartbeat until it shattered, scattering the remaining sunfire essence all over its descendants below. It fell to them, touching down upon them like glitter on their skin, melding with them and nourishing them, and she witnessed their rejuvenation.

Jo gathered up the shadow people in a net of their own soul strings and escorted them to the Sunfire King. They whispered lies to her; they whispered threats and fears and discouraging words, all of which dissolved in the light around them. When they made no headway with her, they began to turn on themselves, bickering and fighting, and thrashing.

"My King," Josie called out to The Sunfire King, having flown as close to his heat and brightness as she could bear to.

"My Beloved Guardian! Oh, Great Sunfire Keeper," he responded, his voice a thundering melody all around her. He sounded nothing like Hazel. "You've brought me The Shadow People. *Thank you*. I will take them into the light, so they can do no more harm. When my radiance has burned away their darkness, and reduced them to renewed beings, we will raise them here to be creatures who make their own happiness instead of trying to take it away from others."

"You can do that, Sunfire King?" Josie asked.

"The light does that. The light restores all beings to their true selves. It's why the shadow creatures run from it and fight against it. They can't stay evil if the light dissolves their darkness. Once they're restored, they'll be like babies: ready for being taken care of and taught better. We will guide them into becoming caring fae folk. Maybe they will even grow up to be Guardians of The Fae. Thank you, Josie."

With that, they were gone. The Shadow People had disappeared in the arms of The Sunfire King. The day shone down, sunny and clear and bright, under a normal, perfectly restored sun.

Down below, Jo realized, after having been a little stunned by the King, the fae folk sang:

We give thanks for the sun in the sky

We give thanks for the light in our hearts

We bathe in the joy of our lives

And grow as one in the warmth

Jo watched flower bushes quickly fill with blossoms and bumblebees, and tree folk dance their branches in proclamations of "hello" and "hooray!" She saw brand new Sunfire babies smile at their mothers, and mermaids dive up from the lake and flip into the air. People ran to each other to embrace in hugs and jumping and joyful crying. She saw Olive and Chloe below, reuniting with their true people. They had the light back. They had their king back. They had their families back.

Family! Hazel! Oh no, I forgot Hazel!

Josie quickly turned and flew back over all the villages to Hazel in the woods. She set down on the ground, separating from her glorious bird friend, Sunshine, and she ran to her brother.

"Hazel! Hazel, wake up, it's me!" But he didn't. He was alive, she could tell, but he was unconscious. Jo couldn't get him to come to. She shook him, gently. She hugged him and kissed his face. But he lay still. He was breathing and he was warm, thank goodness.

As Jo sat pondering what to do next, worrying about both the Sunfire King *and* Grandma Ruby not being there to help her when she needed it, she heard a soft *crunch, crunch* sound coming from behind the trees ahead of her. A small creature was walking on the bed of leaves, in her direction. Was that also the sound of purring?

"Mew." She heard coming from behind a tree. "Meeoww."

Wait. Jo thought. *What is that . . .*

that sounds like . . . Honey?!

Her cat, Honey, sauntered out from behind the tree and smiled.

"Well, now I've seen *everything*. How did you get here? What are you doing here? You couldn't have followed us all this way." Before she could stand up to go pet Honey and work on a plan for getting all three of them home, Honey spoke.

"Please don't move, Josie." Honey stood on her hind legs. She had spoken English, like Josie, but with an accent that Josie had never heard in her life. Josie felt herself become a little dizzy with surprise.

"What..." was all Josie could bring herself to mutter.

"I'm going to show you my true form, now. Don't be afraid. I won't hurt you." Honey began to grow and stretch and completely shed her fur.

This is what Grandma Ruby failed to mention -I knew there was something she was holding back! In our many long talks, our lessons, our trials, our learning about the history of the fae folk and the Sunfire people, she didn't bother to tell me that my cat is a freakin' D R A G O N. Josie stared, and scooted back a ways, in complete awe. Honey was gorgeous as a dragon, Josie thought, as she watched her incredible transformation unfold.

"Dragons are grand shapeshifters, of course." Honey said casually, like it was something everybody already knew. "My people need your help, Josie. I'm here to help you return Hazel to your parents, and then I need you to come with me. May I ask that of you? I will continue to be your companion and protector, afterward, of course, as a ..." she cleared her throat, "*house cat.* That is what Grandma Ruby has assigned me to do, and, well, let's be honest . . . I've come to love being a part of your family."

Josie blinked and shook her head to snap herself out of how shocked and dazed she felt. Her cat ... or ... *DRAGON* was enormous. She was a bright, earthy peach color, with eyes that looked like liquid gold was swimming around a long, reptilian pupil in the center. Her calm breath sparked little specks of flames that went out before they made it to the ground. Her breath produced an extra layer of muggy warmth all around her and it smelled like sunbathing on the earth after it had just rained. It smelled like embers in the fireplace at home. Or fireworks and toasted marshmallows. It smelled like cliffside boulders on a scorching hot day. It smelled like flowers and cinnamon. Sunshine flew to her shoulder and sang an emphatic birdsong *YESSS* to Honey's request for help.

"I guess we're in!" Josie laughed. Would the surprises ever end? She hoped not, deep in her heart. She had not yet had her fill of new and magickal adventures. She could feel it all the way to her bones that she was only just getting started. "But where are my parents?" She eyed Honey's shimmering scales and long, immense talons. "You said we can return Hazel to them?"

"That's what I'm here to do," she purred. Wow, dragon purring was *vastly different* from cat purring! The trees around them shook, just a little. Birds and wildlife grew quiet for a moment, then went back to celebrating life. "May I explain, Beloved Keeper of the Sunfire Folk?" Josie blushed at the mention of her new title, feeling too honored by it to question it.

"Please do." Josie got up and stepped a little closer, her head tilted back to best be able to see all of Honey's large dragon head.

"Excellent. Climb aboard," Honey bowed down to make it easier for Josie.

"Climb aWHAT?" Josie startled.

"Grab Hazel and climb my back. You'll see you both fit comfortably and securely between my scales. They'll keep you warm and safe while I fly us home to your house. I've already returned your parents. We've kept them safe, this whole time, but I believe you had already dreamed that, yes?" Jo nodded at Honey.

"They won't remember anything, Josie," Honey continued. "Neither will Hazel, now that the Sunfire King has left his body. Neither will your neighbors or anyone else . . . you are the only human who will ever know what happened. You'll have access to the memories we've given them -they should already be available to your mind- but you will also retain the accurate ones. They must never know the truth."

Jo s*aw* the validity of Honey's sentiment and agreed to keep everything a secret from her family and from all of humankind. It was necessary to keep the fae safe. So, Josie scooped up her heavy, eight-year-old brother, found a secure niche in Honey's back scales for them both, cradled Sunshine under her shirt, and up they flew toward their parents' home.

Chapter Nine

Josie was astonished by her parents being home as if they'd never been gone, and living as if nothing had ever happened to their family. Hazel lived this new reality, too. Their father was still a firefighter, their mother was still a kindergarten teacher, and Hazel was just like Jo had always known him to be -minus any issues with becoming too cold. They really had been saved from remembering what they'd all been through. They were happy. They were . . . *normal.*

For Hazel and his parents, two years had gone by since Jo had left the house, looking for Grandma Ruby. Hazel was 10, on their return from the Realms of the Fae, and Josie was 18. In their new reality, Grandma Ruby's nieces, Olive and Chloe, had gifted Jo the cottage when they moved away. Jo worked for Ruby at the bookstore and was planning on attending college soon. Hazel was wanting to become a veterinarian, when he grew up. He had become especially fond of birds.

She sat at their table, no fire in the fireplace, sunshine pouring in through the windows, having a sandwich and a glass of milk. She inhaled the aromas that had come back to life, now that her parents were home. She listened to them speak and laugh as if it were the most perfect sound on Earth. It was. But she knew the dragon people needed her. And she knew her parents would still be here when she returned.

So, Jo dropped her brother off at home, gave her mom and dad the biggest hugs she could muster, squeezing some surprise into them, and told them she was going home to her cottage. Honey purred at her ankles.

"I'm bringing Honey with me, okay?" Jo asked, picking up her cat.

"Of course. We'll see you Sunday for family dinner?" Mom smiled. Oh, how Josie had missed this. Her heart sang pure happiness. She heard Sunshine outside on the front porch singing along with her.

"I wouldn't miss it for the world!" Jo beamed.

"Don't forget your keys," Dad said, handing her a full key ring: home, work, and car keys. *Oh my goodness, I have my own car*? Suddenly, knowing washed over her. Jo knew how to drive, now.

"I sure love you all. I'll see you Sunday!" One more hug for everyone and it was time to go. She wanted more time with her family, but it would have to wait. The dragons needed her.

Honey agreed to one more stop: Jo needed to check out her new home. They drove up the main street, veered left past the bookstore, and found the off road to the cottage, with Honey and Sunshine sitting contently in the passenger seat of Jo's little white pick-up truck.

Jo pulled her truck to a full stop in the grass near her new house. They all got out and walked (Sunshine flew) to the front door of Jo's home. Had it always been this pale sage green color? Her home looked so pretty in the full daylight. The smell of her front yard's lavender embraced her in a cloud of sweetness. *I'm home.* The house key let them in.

Jo's heart melted. Most of Olive and Chloe's things were gone and they had been replaced by her own belongings. She noticed a bookcase in the living room, lined with all of her favorite childhood books from Grandma Ruby's bookstore. Her family table and chairs were here – she hadn't noticed the different set at her parents' house. A framed picture of her and her brother hung on the wall by the front door. And the art from her old bedroom decorated the walls of her living room, now.

Her kitchen window was overflowing with the many houseplants from before, all soaking up the abundant rays of sunshine. Dried herbs lined the walls – a knowing that Grandma Ruby would teach her how to use them came over her. The air smelled like vanilla sugar cookies. She saw jarred tea leaves and honey, goodies from the garden, and a new bread baking machine. She took a drink of cold, clean water from the kitchen faucet.

Finally, Jo poked her head into her bedroom. It was just as she had left it. Hazel's scarf lay on top of the bedding where they had slept, that first night. She picked it up and smelled it. It was missing . . . something, but it was still an amazing reminder of their adventure together. She held it to her cheek, grateful for the amazing connection she had with her brother, filled with memories he would now never recall. She draped his scarf across the oak bookshelf in the corner of her bedroom as a beloved decoration to always remind her what they had gone through – a reminder of everything and everyone they had saved.

She turned and saw Honey waiting patiently for her in the hallway.

"I'm ready. Do I need to bring anything?" Jo asked her.

"No, my dear. We will have everything we need. Let's head out to the garden. We'll go to my people through the orchard. Make sure you grab another coin from the fountain. Those always seem to come in handy." Honey's tail twitched.

"They're magickal aren't they?" Jo asked.

"Quite. They're gateways. I'll tell you all about it on our flight." Honey grinned.

My skin rippled with goosebumps.

Out back, the garden thrived vibrantly. Sunshine flapped her happy wings in the fountain pool. Honey moved to the back of the garden to expand into her full, ginormous dragon form. Then Jo and Sunshine climbed her back and found their safe niche. Honey's skin, between her scales, felt like leather, but was shiny and impenetrable like diamonds. She radiated heat, which warmed them as they flew through the high skies.

On their way, after flying through the realms of the fae, for quite a while, they approached a large lake that seemed to go on for miles. It caught Jo's attention when the waters began to shake. Small waves rolled out as a figure started emerging from the deep. They circled far above. As the figure became clear, Jo gasped. It was Grandma Ruby . . . but about the size of a 50-foot statue. She rose up from the water, every animal and fae creature in the area, galloping, crawling, flying, pouring forth to see her. White light rolled off of her in every direction. They all sang out in unison, loudly enough that it echoed in Josie's ears, "Gaaaiiiaaaa!"

The sound rang out beautifully and enveloped everyone and everything nearby. "Gaaaaiiiiiaaaa," they sang, welcoming and honoring their Goddess.

Gaia, Keeper of the Fae Forest looked up at Jo and waved with a smile. Jo was shaken by her brilliance. Had she missed how stunning Gaia was, when she had last seen her? Or had Gaia kept it to herself? Snapping herself out of her daze, Jo saw Zhera flying toward them. *We are here to take Zhera with us,* Jo *saw.* Then Zhera shifted. Her feathers began to vanish as her wings and torso extended.

Zhera slipped from raven form into an immaculate, black, shimmering dragon and she flew up alongside them.

"Hello," she grinned at Josie. She winked one of her sparkling purple eyes at her. Honey and Zhera purred.

"NOW, we're ready," Honey said. "Oh. Actually, Jo, there is one more thing you should know."

"What's that?" Jo was still stunned by Zhera's exquisite transformation – her strength and power and beauty – the ease with which she moved and flew her enormous, muscular body, after having just been in raven form. So, this was Gaia's secret, then? Gaia worked with dragons.

"My name," Honey said. "My *dragon name* is Wynterburn. Honey is just my housecat name."

"What!" Jo shouted. "Of course! *Of course* you would have a name besides the one I gave you when you came to live with us as a housecat. How have I not thought of this? Wow, your dragon name is so pretty."

"You need to know this, Josie," Wynterburn continued, "because no one will call me Honey, where we're going. But also because my power resides in my name. You can call on me by my name, even silently, and I will come to you almost instantly. Please remember that. We'll be there soon."

Josie saw the skyline change drastically in the distance. Through what seemed to be a glimmering, transparent portal, volcanic rock shot up, miles tall. Fire erupted and cascaded from their spiky points. A black tear in the red sky loomed over the dragon world below, slowly dripping something tar-like upon it. Jo *saw* what they were up against and began to call forth all her strength and magick.

Saving the Dragon beings was going to be quite a task. *Fortunately,* she thought to herself in all knowing, *I was made for this.* She stretched her magnificent yellow wings, noticing it create a stronger glide for Winterburn beneath her, and set into flight on her own, singing a powerful birdsong chant to call forth the forces of good in their favor.

Half a dozen of the Sunfire people flew to their sides, filling the sky with light as they headed to Wynterburn's home. Fairies surrounded them, wings flickering in the wind. Elemental beings extended their magick to them from below. A mountain waved in the distance. The Fae Folk joined in with them, in every way they could. In solidarity with the dragons and in gratitude for Josie's return to the sun, the Fae Folk lent her their magick. Jo knew, then: *Unity is power. Unity brings healing. Unity restores us. It's time.*

THE END.

FOR NOW.

ABOUT THE AUTHOR

Lindsay Swanberg grew up on the shores of California, and moved north to Oregon in 2002, after backpacking around Kaua'i Hawaii for several adventurous and nomadic months. Raising her two beautiful children, she set up shop as a preschool child care owner and teacher, and has been fulfilling her passion of working with children and families ever since.

Lindsay has her degree, with an extra year of studies in child development, education, and family studies, and a two-year diploma in medicinal herbalism and holistic health. She is additionally a Reiki Master Teacher and Nichiren Buddhist. Lindsay loves traveling, nature, animals, good food, connecting with friends, and live music. She believes that well-being is at the core of a happy life, no matter our age.

Lindsay has been writing her heart out for years.

You can find her many other books at
www.LindsaySwanberg.com

Other Books by the Author

Adventure of the Water Walker

-

The Day Robert Became a Monster

-

A Movement of Courage: Connecting More Deeply for a Happier Life

-

Wholesome Parenting: Paving a Brighter and Kinder Future with Our Children

-

How to Start & Maintain Your Own Successful Child Care Business

-

Willow Song: A Book of Poetry

-

Underneath the Sparrow Tree

-

Beneath the Within: A Book of Poetry

Printed in Great Britain
by Amazon